I am Helpful

RODALE KiDS

It is going to be
a great day.

Mom and Dad are bringing
my new baby sister
home today.
I can't wait!

I help Grandma get
the twins up.
All dressed.

Breakfast served.

Teeth brushed.

Ready for baby!
Grandma tells me
that I am helpful.

At last, they are home.
Baby Emily looks bigger
and cuter than she did
in the hospital!
Mom looks tired.
She looks so happy, too.

I know what to do.
I help Dad unpack.

While Mom rests, Grandma shows me how to hold Emily. Sometimes we give Emily a bottle.

I even help change
her diaper.
Pee-yew!

The days fly by.
Soon Grandma goes
home to Grandpa.
It's up to me to be
Mom and Dad's helper.
I've got this.

Sometimes it is
all about Emily.

Sometimes it is
all about the twins.
They can make
a lot of noise.

And then Emily
makes a lot of noise!
I know what to do.

We can go outside
to play.

14

Or we can stay inside
and read.
I am helpful.

Sometimes I want
it to be all about me.
Math can be tricky.
And Mom is really
good at it.

But Emily is teething.
So Mom has
her hands full.

Dad is busy, too.
He is putting
the twins to bed.

18

I figure it out.
Helping myself
is another way
to be helpful.

We take a trip to visit
Grandma and Grandpa.
It is Grandpa's birthday.

Emily is excited.

She is crawling
everywhere.

Finally, it is
party time.
I help in the kitchen.

Then I set the table.

Now it is
time to eat!

Happy Birthday Grandpa

I put Emily
in her high chair.
Then I set up her food.

There is so much good food to eat! Everyone is talking and laughing.

Emily wants to join in.
She has something to say.
She blurts out a word.

It is her first word.
Everyone stops eating.
We look at Emily.
Emily looks at us.

She points to me
and says "June!"
She said my name!

I love my family.
It feels good
to help when I can.
I am helpful.

When do
YOU
feel helpful?

Can you think of
three examples?